Purrfect

Purrfect

Aislynn Cross & Mia Cicilia

2019

First Printing: May 2019

Dedication

To my incredible and creative book buddy, Mia

Contents

Prologue

As our paws crossed the threshold, the first chapter in our lives had begun.

***

The day we were born, fireworks crashed through the sky. It was the Fourth of July and the sky glowed vibrantly. I don't remember how we met the horrible, mad scientist but I wish we never did. He was our first owner.

"Kittens!" he boomed, and we came to his feet like puppies, "Today we have a very special treat for you: scraps." I hiss angrily at him, scrunching up my nose.

"You are little monsters. That's what you are," he continued coyly, "or at least what you will be after today." He laughed maniacally to himself. We all shook with fear.

***

"Or at least you will be." The words reverberated through my head. What was that supposed to mean?

I remember the marble tiles on the floor of his lab, how he kept us apart from each other, separated by thick cages like lab rats. I remember a lot from back then. Funny because we were all so young. I can remember the noxious smell of sterilized equipment and how our food glowed green. I remember how it tasted too. When I tasted the neon mush, my face puckered up and it was bitter. As soon as a bite was swallowed down, I could feel the food trying to come back up, but I had to eat it. Regardless of taste, however, food is still food, right?

***

After a few days of isolation, I began to hear voices and seeing things. I could hear my own thoughts, and see the world around me, but I could also hear what sounded like my sister's voice. It scared me. The man with a clipboard in hand and lab coat falling off of his thin frame walked into her room and I could feel her shaking.

"So it seems that your treatment was a success, and you have the power of super strength." She looked at her paws. "I'll call you Muscles," he laughed to himself. Tears welled up in her eyes, blurring her sight. She just wanted to be a baby kitten.

It was like the page of a children's book had turned and I was in a new scene. This time a different sister. "So it seems that your treatment was a success, and you have the power of super stretch. Your name will be Rubber."

He made his rounds, again and again. "Your treatment was a success, and you have the power of lightning. Your name is now Bolt."

"Your treatment was a success, you have the power of laser eyes. Your lasers are red and so is your name: Red."

All of his responses conjoined into one heap. Finally, my turn came, and I prepared myself for the worst. Nothing came. Looking at me with a saddened expression, “Your treatment wasn’t a success...”

I stopped listening to him. I felt like the outcast of my family, a part of me wanted to be special and wanted to be different; unique like them. I knew that I was different, that my powers just weren’t visible to him. I could see into other people’s minds feel what they felt, see what they saw, hear what they heard. What I didn’t know was just how valuable my powers would end up to be.

My sisters and I live in a brown cardboard box. It's a box with the lid taped open wide. Our journey began in a lab and led us to the side of a road in the bitter autumn wind. I'm too little to look over, but I can look up.

Maybe the lid being opened wasn't the greatest choice, I think to myself as the drizzle poured down. I can feel my fur growing colder by the minute. Sitting huddled with the others for warmth, I can see the flashing of vibrant blue and red. The wailing of blaring sirens racing slowly along the boulevard makes my little heart race. "Won't they quiet down already?" Muscles whines.

We were all shaking from the autumn cold, but eventually the sun rose, and with it hope of warmth and hope of a new home. I woke up to the sound of birds carrying a tune of cheer. Maybe that was part of my power; the power to understand their melodies.

"Hey, what are they singing about?" Rubber teases.

"How cold it is!" I blurt out. She laughs for a short while then starts to nod off.

I can't sleep. I won't sleep. There is too much to see and too much to hear. Yellow and orange leaves fall around me. One yellow leaf flutters down to Red's nose. She sneezes and sends a red-hot laser crashing into the side of the box. My sisters were all asleep, dreaming and muttering to themselves, but that jolt of energy had them all standing at attention.

***

"Meow!" Pink grubby hands reached into our box and lift me up.

From up here, I can see the heads of people bobbing around, some little children stealing a glance at us, their parents dragging them away by the hand.

"You don't belong here," the girl with frizzy pigtails said as she poked and prodded at the box labeled Free Kittens.

A woman, with hair pinker than the young girl's coat, crowded around the box. Her earrings were like pendants, long and swaying. I try to touch one with my paws and miss. She laughs and stands up placing the weight of our box under her arm and starts to walk. Our heads began to bob, colliding with each other like a set of Newton's Cradle.

"Stop bumping around! You're going to break!" The woman laughs.

I'm glad she found us; she's kind. Much kinder than the man that dumped us on that ice-cold corner. Our fur is not soft and fuzzy like it was yesterday or the day before, and our stomachs all growl with passion.

The woman must have heard our talkative stomachs, so she said, "Don't you worry; we've got plenty of snacks at home for you."

As the woman walked through the red threshold, the warmth from inside wraps around us. My goosebumps begin to relax as she places our box on the ground, and says, “Oh! You’re all so precious!” and scurries out the door. “Be good kitties, now. I’m going out for a moment to get some more blankets. Bye!”

“Wait, sis!” The little girl in pink pigtails runs after her. The door slams behind them.

***

We divide and conquer our new environment, spreading out and taking on different rooms. I head to my favorite place; the kitchen. I leap from countertop to countertop, hopping to the tallest table where a dish of milk sits unattended. The blood-curdling scream of Red reverberates in my mind, it knocks me off balance and sends me crashing to the floor. No time for milk now. I sprint through rooms, searching for her, calling out her name, but I can tell that she is too scared to answer. I take a second to regroup myself, try to see her surroundings from her perspective. It feels like I’m invading her privacy but I have no choice. She’s terrified and I need to know why. Then I know. I know why she screamed but was too scared to make a sound.

“SNAKE!” I cry so loud even the next city over can hear it. “Snake! In the bathroom!” I try to stay calm, but I’m terrified as well.

"Coming!" Bolt shouts boldly.

"Same here!" Rubber joins.

***

Since that fateful day, I've always been able to see other beings' dreams. I can see from their perspectives, and I can read their minds. It scared me at first because I always know what they are thinking, so they can never lie to me. I guess that that's a good thing, but it can be bothersome, and, for some reason, I also feel comfort. We're all scared, but we all want to save Red, and nothing will stop us from achieving that goal.

***

We all come into the room ready to defeat the snake. I can see prey encased in a heavy, light-white body. The rat is already gone, and it makes me sad and angry. Tears well up in my eyes and my heart mourns for the rat.

"Why...Why can't snakes just be vegan?" Rubber mutters meekly under her breath.

"Why don't you tell me?" The snake replies coyly.

He loosens his grip on the rat and lunges forward toward Rubber. She's stagnant and motionless, like a tree. Just then, a zap of light soars through the air, bounding past the head of the beast, singeing off a corner of a hanging towel.

I see a barrage of images race through my mind. The images are memories, but they're not mine, they're his. I guess that this must be my power; the power to read minds, and I can see his life flash before his eyes. It's like a puzzle piece falling into place. He's not a monstrous villain like the mad scientist, his memories are full of warmth and hope and joy. He has a cold air about him, but he's kind deep down.

The snake backs away defeated.

"Hey," I say in a soft, genuine tone.

"Hey?" Bolt replies.

The snake sighs, he's partially confused and partially relieved.

"Seems like we got off to a bad start; I'm Nick." He flashes the tag around his neck.

"I'm…confused, why befriend a snake?" Red stutters.

"He was just teasing you, don't worry. He won't hurt you. Actually, he was hoping that we could maybe be...friends?" I blurt out.

"How did you know what I was thinking?" He asks, dumbfounded.

"It's Jay's power. She can read minds. Cool, right?" Rubber jumps in.

"Sure...um...ok. So will you be my friends?"

"Sure!" Red exclaims immediately.

"Really?"

"Of course." We all reply in unison.

"So why do you little ones have powers?"

"It's a long story."

***

"Hey guys, I was wondering, could we maybe keep our powers a secret from them?" Little Red asks softly.

"Why?" I replied.

"I just feel...I just feel like the humans won't like it very much; like they'll abandon us too."

"I agree with Red they could get scared of us."

"It's best to keep it secret," Rubber chimes in.

"Ok then, it's settled. You got that Nick?"

"Don't worry, my lips are sealed," he replied.

"Good."

Red's imagination is always filled with light. She thinks of the night sky and feels comfort, and she looks to the stars every night, mesmerized by the endlessness of it. Red is my own little star, and I see a sea of darkness filled with small orbs of shimmering light. It's stunning.

"Red, are you daydreaming about stars again?"

"Can't you see how pretty they are?"

"It's the middle of the day."

"But still…"

"You are staring into the sun."

"I feel like you're judging me."

"I am."

We laughed for a few minutes and then Red strayed into the kitchen, lost in thought. Her imagination never ceases to bewilder me.

As for the others, all of their minds are focused on one thing. One magical, beautiful thing. T.V. There's one show that they all seem to love. I love it too. *Aliens.* There's an alien from the moon. When the humans start to invade, she has to lead a rebellion to fight against it. When the humans land, they take over, replacing her civilization's flag with their own, and eat her cheese. The first act of her rebellion was to stop all of the human's communication with the outsiders. So she jabbed a stick into the ignition spot of their shuttle and it exploded! I don't know what's going to happen next, but I have to wait an entire week to find out what happens to her. It's so unfair! Oh, and my favorite part; the alien has an alien cat named Lola, who was born on The Fourth of July! Just like the five of us.

Muscles, however, is obsessed with a different show which airs at the same time, so it's hard not to fight over the remote.

***

"The remote is mine! I have to know what happens next."

"No, it's ours!"

"Three against one! That's not a fair fight, Rubber, and you know it!"

"Two against one. Don't involve me in this, Muscles," I say harshly.

"That was rude." She scoffs, "Ok, even if it's two against one; It's still not a fair fight!"

"Ha ha! We got it, Muscles! Come and get it," Rubber taunts from a few meters high.

"Ok."

She powerfully lunges forward to grab the remote with her teeth. Success! Bolt angrily starts to conduct energy, ready for a strike against the remote thief, but Red stops them in their tracks firing a warning zap between the two of them. Except the warning shot doesn't miss entirely. We all turn toward the smell of burning hair to see a wide-eyed woman with pink hair and her jaw dropped open.

So much for keeping our powers a secret.

We all freeze, expecting the worst. But nothing happens. Instead, her hand clasps over her dropped jaw.

"Sis! That was so cool!" The silence was broken by the little girl with brown pigtails.

"You're right, it was cool," she said as she bent over and began to clean up the mess that we had made.

She pointed at us with a quivering finger and said, "No lasers in the house, please." We all nodded our heads in shocked agreement.

***

When Rubber emerged from the kitchen, Pirate's Booty dust stuck to her paws, and vanilla ice cream residue was spread across her smiling cheeks. I knew that the greatest food combination in history had just been created. I've never seen my sister Rubber do anything but smile. She is a little ball of spirit, with the pastel patterns and markings to prove it. Sometimes I feel that she would fit better in a carnival, rather than in a crowded city capital. I look through her perspective and see a vibrant mind bursting at the seams with colour.

***

Rubber has always loved to paint. She dips her little paws into the paint buckets and the paint swirls it around, making a marbled pattern in the bucket. Her paw drips with the concoction as she dips, again and again, entranced by the pattern she creates. Her paws soak up the pink and blue and yellow pigments. Sometimes we joke that she's half paint, half kitten.

With both paws covered in wet paint she walks down the stairs to the dark and carpeted basement. She carries the dripping bucket of paint all the way down too. *Drip, drop*. Every other stair brings a new big *drip* or tiny *drop*. She reaches the bottom of the stairs and puts the bucket down, looking at her new canvas.

Her jaw is sore and tired from carrying the weight of the bucket, which was almost as big as her, weighing twice as much. She looks at her trail of painted paw prints that lead down the stairs and she smiles. The stairs are no longer a boring beige like they were a few minutes ago. Her trip has made them a vibrant mix of greens and pink. She dips her paw into the bucket and smears the paint across her cheeks. She looks like a warrior, and at that moment, I know she feels empowered like a warrior as well.

She didn't care that she would later be in trouble, she was proud of her soon-to-be masterpiece. She looked once more at her blank canvas. A canvas of possibility, she thought. It was a long, large egg-white wall. Bare. She takes a dip and begins to reach as high as she can. As I watch her from behind the pillar in the room, I am in awe as the entire wall becomes covered in paint. Effortlessly, the 6-foot wall had been coated in a thick layer of blues and purples and pinks.

“Eeek!” She spotted me and jumped back into the wall behind her. Her back coat was now covered in the tacky, colourful paint.

“You didn’t see any of that did you.”

“Yeah, the humans are going to be furious,” I laughed.

As she stood back to admire her work, her smile began to glow even brighter.

“I like it,” I say in awe.

“Me too.”

"Hello Kittens! I have gathered you all here to present you with an opportunity, an opportunity to become the greatest superheroes this world has ever seen. So what do you say? Will you be part of the Purrfect Protectors," our human proclaimed with such a straight face that we all have no choice but to laugh.

She continues, "This city has seen many dangers, and it will be difficult but I have hope that you will all succeed. Plus, I already made the costumes, and it would be a shame to let them go to waste."

We rolled our eyes, but we all knew it didn't take much convincing to make us a team. In all honesty, we would have done it anyway, but it didn't hurt to have someone there to support us.

***

"Do you mind if I publish a few things about you in the local paper?" We shake our heads side to side like ragdolls. Our names and faces spread across the headlines. Silly titles like, "Are you Kitten me?" began to circulate.

"You're an instant success! The press loves you!" She cheered. "Hey guess what? Today, to commemorate you five, I wanted to cook something special! How does salmon sound?"

Our stomachs all growl in enthusiastic agreement. The sweet smell of salmon wafts into every room of the house. Waiting is agonizing. I am then caught off guard by the *Beep! Beep! Beep!* of an alarm.

Smoke fills the house, followed by a sickly bitter smell. We all suit up into our masks and come to the kitchen to see a mask of smoke covering the oven. Our owner stands waving a previously white towel over the smog.

She explains, “Oh, the salmon still looked pink. I didn’t want it to be raw, but, I guess I overcooked it a little bit.”

On further inspection, the salmon was coal black and hard as stone.

Rubber and I watch TV until the sun goes down. The once luminous screen dims as the sight of smoke and the smell of burning plastic coats the fluorescently lighted room.

We succumb to the fumes, sprint down the fire escape as our limbs cascade into the street. We catch a glimpse of a dog and a squirrel chatting with a robin at the top of a tree.

Mr. McRuff waits cunningly, circling around the tree's base. A small squirrel squirms down the trunk and climbs into its hollow. Mr. McRuff bounds forward launching his paws into the soft and squishy grass beside the tree, and sticks his head into the dark, hollow pit. He sees the squirrel's swollen face, buck teeth, and big eyes.

He growls and nips and barks at the little squirrel, grabbing its tail and ripping it from its home. The squirrel's body is launched to the grass, as he throws his nut and hits Mr. McRuff's eye. The squirrel rushes again to recapture and protect his acorn and leaps to the grassy ground. Mr. McRuff's heart beat slows down as he watches the squirrel grow smaller and smaller until almost fading completely out of sight.

***

We head back to our apartment, the smell of smoke is gone and the TV is back on. Whir! Whir! The sound of a tornado siren screams from the TV screen flashing a red, vibrant ribbon across the screen stating; City Under Attack. City Under Attack. We're taken out of our trance by the sound of shattering glass. Muscles perches on the windowsill and looks out at the grayish city masked by a dark shadow.

"Muscles, what do you think's out there?" Rubber asks leaping onto the windowsill.

"Maybe it's just storm clouds!" Muscles jumps to join them, but falls a little short.

"Ha ha! you missed!" Muscles jeers.

"But I just-" I start to respond.

"No buts, no cuts, no coconuts."

"But"

"You heard me! No buts, no cuts, no coconuts. "

"I"

"No buts no c"

"Will you two quit it already," Red objects. "Look out there."

She waves at the window and taps on the glass. I see the intensity in her eyes and hear the sharpness of her voice, which scares me a little bit. I watch people in cars or running, in shock or terror or both, rushing to to leave town. I guess we're all a little terrified, but not Red. She presses her paw against the window and smoke begins to fill the air. A large chunk of melted window falls to the fire escape.

“Are you coming or not?” She taunts as we all bewilderingly stare into the gaping hole.

“You are going to be in so much trouble,” Nick hisses.

I jump out onto the fire escape first and make my way toward the center of the commotion.

I hear a shy and timid voice mumble, "I'm so scared." The voice puts me on edge as we prepare to fight.

The winds start to pick up and our fur floats in the cold breeze. Our battlefield is wedged between two rows of buildings, each row scraping the sky. In the center stands a great dane of equal size.

"We're not gonna win, we can't," sighs Rubber.

"I don't like it when you start to talk like that. Don't be so pessimistic."

"How do you want me to talk?"

"I don't know, but you're really bringing down the team's spirit."

"You don't know the first thing about team spirit, Muscles."

"Yeah I do, after all, I'm the leader."

"No, you're not."

Red interrupts the two of them saying, "Quiet! You'll give away our positions."

"Too late!" Mr. McRuff scoffs.

We all sprint to find a new place to hide. An endless cycle of sprinting and hiding. The five of us are out of breath, but he hasn't even broken a sweat. Mr. McRuff sticks his big nose right into Red's face. Red zaps him and Mr. McRuff yelps. We all sprint away, but I hear a cry in the far distance. Red is trapped behind Mr.

McRuff's paw. With his mouth, Mr. McRuff picks Red up by the scruff of her silver and grey neck.

"Red!" I scream.

"Still here!" She hollers back. The heavy smog of dog breath clouded around her face making it hard for her to breathe.

Rubber calls out, "Are you okay?"

"Yeah. I'm Okay," she answers with a wide grin plastered on her face. She lied.

I can hear her terrified little voice mumbling in a quiet panic. She's dangling at least two stories high above an impressive crowd. Mr. McRuff sways her to the right and the left, and the captive audience of onlookers gasp.

The commotion had driven most people out of their buildings which was lucky because in one monstrous swing of his paw, Mr. McRuff had toppled them all.

A majestic cityscape flattened in mere moments. Muscles leaps to stop the buildings from collapsing any further, but I can tell that it takes all of her efforts.

"Hey, Muscles, try to tilt the buildings to your left!" Rubber shouts.

"Like this?"

"No, to your other left," says Rubber, slightly exasperated.

"Oh, you mean like this?"

The wobbling buildings stabilize and the weight becomes more bearable. People still in the buildings are filled with confusion which soon converts to sheer panic.

"Attack!" Screams Bolt as she launches toward Mr. McRuff. Her body becomes charged with electricity and a thunderous boom vibrates through the air as Bolt collides with Mr. McRuff.

It knocks Mr. McRuff back a few steps and sends Bolt plummeting to the roadway below. She's out of breath, but victorious. Red slips from his mouth and lands on the ground. Tears well up in her eyes and she has to take a second to collect herself before she heads back to regroup. We all smile relieved that she's safe.

Red says, “You’re on fire, Bolt.”

“I know,” he says patting himself on the back.

“No. Your tail’s on fire.”

Red points at Bolt with her silver-gray paw. Bolt’s orange fur turns white. It was as if she had seen a ghost. She runs to extinguish it and leaps into the lake.

***

I hear a loud crack and see a pipe burst near Muscle’s feet. She slips and the buildings come cascading gracefully down as her legs give way. She sprints away in time, however, not fast enough to evade Mr. McRuff’s round of auxiliary attacks. Muscles inches away to a safe and protected area shaded by trees and rests.

“One down, four more to go,” Mr. McRuff announces. The people crowding the street gasp.

Rubber wraps her body around Mr. McRuff’s legs and tries to trip him, but her attempts are futile. No matter what she does, he easily escapes her traps.

“Round after round after round...does it ever end?” Rubber wines.

I can see her limbs starting to tremble and strain. She can’t keep fending off the medley of attacks.

“Three against one.” Mr. McRuff announces as Rubber trips over her own trap and spirals into the lake.

It sounds like the beginning of an underdog story where the protagonist fights three on one and wins in the end. I can't let that happen.

Red shoots her lasers at him from afar, but after a few minutes of constant shots, her eyes tire and she needs to take a break. He takes his opportunity, and in one swipe of his paw has her pinned against the row of collapsed buildings.

"Two against one," he roars.

Bolt finishes climbing out of the lake and cleaning herself off, but her fur is still damp and charred. She can't produce any electricity and is immediately knocked down. His sharp claw crashes through the roof of an unoccupied car; triggering it's incessant alarm.

"One against one, I'm starting to like these odds." He kicks the car into the side of the toppled buildings and stands triumphant.

I see myself being thrown across the rough pavement, collapsing in defeat. It's a disastrous ending; five kittens defeated, lying motionless on the ground.

“We’re not done yet,” I mumble through gritted teeth. Pulling myself up.

“What was that little one?” Mr. McRuff says degradingly.

“I said. We're not done yet!” I shout at the top of my lungs.

I hold my head up high like I’m wearing a crown. I’m ready to face the Goliath.

***

“You think you’re so tough?” Mr. McRuff jeers. “I’m not scared to show up a bunch of baby kittens.”

“We’re not weak. Nobody’s bringing us down,” I shout.

The others begin to rouse slowly. We couldn’t defeat him alone, but maybe as a team, we can. Rubber and Bolt work together to create a slingshot, firing a charged canon into Mr. Mcruff’s stomach. He’s knocked to the ground. Red and Bolt zap at his feet so he can’t stand. Muscles pins Mr. Mcruff under two buildings, and slowly he begins to shrink. The world is silent and calm. The stillness is eerie.

I scream, "You are hereby banished from this city!"

Then I hear the meek squeak I had heard before the battle started. So tiny and small.

Whimpering, "Sorry." The voice was quiet and timid, much like my own.

I look around trying to find the source of the sound, but I can't. As Mr. McRuff shrinks, I realize that the shy voice I recognize is his. He's crying out, and for the first time, I take a second to collect my thoughts. I feel pity for the city that's devastated, pity for the terrified civilians caught up in our drama and pity for him. Pity for the poor pup whose eyes are glazed over like blown glass. Seemingly begging for help.

I hear him speak once more, and my tiny heart sinks to the ground when I hear him say, "All I wanted to do was find friends to play with."

So many thoughts should be rushing through my mind. Thoughts of victory, and of success, but all I can think about is how much I want to help him, and how much we all need to help the poor and innocent soul behind that voice.

He picks himself up and growls at the others meanly. Red zaps at his feet and the battle continues. I can't wrap my brain around the situation. I hide behind a tree to take shelter from the constant attacks coming my way.

If he wants friends, then why is he trying to kill us all? I take a deep breath and submerge myself into his memory. I shudder when I see the face of the mad scientist. Was he a victim just like us? I can hear the coy voice of the scientist's laugh. Is this why? Why he's attacking the city?

As I peer further, I can see nothing but gray. He's friendless and lonely. The only person he has is his owner, the mad scientist.

I go out and try to approach him, but his paw collides with my face and sends me sprawling once again. I brush myself off, stare into his eyes, and realize the true extent of my powers. If I focus hard enough I can predict his moves, right? It works! I can dodge his attacks!

"Nice job Jay," Muscles cheers from underneath her stack of buildings.

"You go girl!" Red shouts.

A chant starts, "Let's go Jay! Let's go Jay!" Their voices keep me moving.

Muscles slips from under her buildings which come crashing down onto Mr. Mcruff, trapping him under their heavy weight.

Chapter 11: Not So Ruff After All

We all pant like dogs, dirty and tired and sore. We have accomplished so much, and it feels good to win the battle. Rubber uncoiles herself and Muscle returns the city's buildings to their positions like fallen dominoes. My palms still hurt from being thrown across the street.

With the last bit of might I have, I say, "I'll be your friend."

My siblings look at me as if I am crazy. I don't care. I need to save him. He seems so sad and so defenseless. Now, for the first time, I see who he truly is. Not as an evil and savage being with sharp teeth and dog breath, but an innocent animal longing for any act of kindness shown towards him.

"You're welcome to join our team," I offered. His head jolts toward me.

The other kittens object, but I shush them and continue.

"You must start learning the ways of good. I think a good place to start would be with not tormenting the entire city."

Rubber begins to smile, and comments, "Maybe explain yourself too?"

Mr. McRuff begins his long, woeful tale, "I doubt you'd believe me, it seems a little bit far fetched."

"I see what you did there," I laugh.

Red shushes, "Jay, now is not the time for puns, this is serious."

Mr. McRuff continues, "I don't remember much, but I've been like this for as long as I can remember. It all started back in a lab with a malicious man in a white lab coat and glowing food…"

It didn't take long for us to realize that we share the same childhood trauma, and the same common enemy.

"What's your name," Red questions, trying to dissipate the heavy atmosphere.

"Mr. McRuff," he replies tentatively.

"So, Mr. McRuff, do you wan't to be friends?" Muscles questions.

"Let's save the world while we're at it too!" Rubber chimes in.

"Friends?" I say with a smile spreading from ear to ear.

"Friends!" He smiles.

As the sun sets, we start to walk to our apartment building, to where our owner lives. We all realize that he was not the same dangerous dane that attacked the city. We chose a life of adventure and heroism, five kittens and a great dane united against a common enemy, the mad scientist. A hurricane of unanswered questions about our past and our future echo wildly through each of our minds, but we all knew without a shadow of a doubt, that as our paws crossed the threshold, the next chapter in our lives had begun.

Rachel Gopalani; for editing this book.

Mother; for supporting and helping me.

Mrs. Wiley; for always challenging me.

Mia; when you make up your mind, no one and nothing can stand in your way. Always stay determined and strong